Praise for Francis Levy's *The*

"Francis Levy has an unhampered, endearingly maverick imagination—as if Donald Barthelme had met up with Maimonides and together they decided to write about the world as it appeared to them. These deceptively simple and parable-like stories are full of wily pleasures and irreverent wisdom about everything from the failure of insight to make anything happen, to the subtle gratifications of friendship, to the tragicomedy of eros."
—**Daphne Merkin**, author of *This Close to Happy*
     and *22 Minutes of Unconditional Love*

"A collection of bleak and amusing literary short stories from Levy...A dark, sometimes funny, meditation on the absurd trials of life."
—*Kirkus Reviews*

"Francis Levy's fiction is knowing but never instructive. His characters inhabit a twilight zone where the lines blur between dream and waking, familiar and surreal, inevitability and surprise. These short takes, snapshots of feelings-in-flight, of moments still being formed, build an irresistible magic. I found myself enchanted."
—**Rocco Landesman**, Broadway producer and former Chairman
     of the National Endowment for the Arts

"*The Kafka Studies Department* is not about academia. It's about anomie, and how complicated it is to figure out what's really going on with people. Of course (since it's Levy) it's about sex. Kafka's shadow is everywhere as Levy's characters stumble their way through their compromised lives. The interlinked stories leap across time and context, in satisfying and sometimes hilariously poetic ways."
—**David Kirkpatrick**, journalist and author of *The Facebook Effect*

"A startling collection of thirty literary gems deftly illustrated by Hallie Cohen into dreamy sketches, which perfectly suit the tone of the work. Initially it seems like these stories are fed into a kind of a magical Kafka Cuisinart where they come out tightly sealed, hilariously ironic, and occasionally mysterious. On the surface they have the muted highbrow narrative of Wes Anderson movies. On a closer look you'll find they are actually far more nuanced and layered. To a lesser writer, they could easily bloat to ten times their size. This economy though, allows for the reader to reflect on each piece—many of which unravel as modern parables that have the makings of mini-masterpieces."
—**Arthur Nersesian**, author of *The Five Books of Moses* and *The Fuck-Up*

— The — Kafka Studies Department

Emotional Mysteries

Francis Levy

Illustrations by Hallie Cohen

Heliotrope Books
New York

Published by
Heliotrope Books,
New York, NY

All rights and publicity information: philoctates@gmail.com

First printing 2023

Paperback ISBN: 978-1-956474-27-5
Hardcover ISBN: 978-1-956474-29-9
E-book ISBN: 978-1-956474-28-2

For Dr. Kafka

Thanks to Christopher O'Brien and Michael Dwyer for their sage publishing and design advice and thanks to John Oakes of *Evergreen Review* for his suggestions and support. I am also grateful to Louise Crawford and Linda Quigley who brought this book into the public eye, to Naomi Rosenblatt of Heliotrope Books for her support and guidance, to Lauren Cerand for her encouragement and to Adam Ludwig for his attention to structure and detail.

Contents

The
Kafka Studies
Department

Martin was your typical Kafka scholar.
Painfully shy with a receding posture...

The
Kafka Studies
Department

All the faculty of the Kafka Studies Department were withdrawn, retiring individuals who'd had troubled relationships with their fathers, and hence authority, all their lives. When you met these rail-thin, bespectacled creatures, most of whom lived alone in the kind of off-campus housing usually reserved for graduate students, there was little question how they had found their master. But the whole is sometimes greater than the sum of its parts. The mere fact of a department devoted to the study of Franz Kafka—the only of its kind in the country—had attracted international attention.

The Kafka Studies Department was perpetually at odds with the university. Someone had to raise money; someone had to deal with an administration more interested in enrollment than excellence; someone had to handle the real world.

None of these gentlemen had the least ability to cope with life. So when the letter arrived announcing a severe cutback in funding, no solution was proposed. Yes, it was a blow at a time when the department's fine reputation should have put it in an exalted position, but no one dared speak up; no one knew how. Further, it was Kafkaesque. The administration was simply an illustration of the irrational malevolence of *The Trial.* They would watch the department deteriorate. Life was imitating art.

There were two students who stood out in the class that entered the year the Kafka Studies Department suffered the cutbacks that threatened its very existence. Martin was your typical Kafka scholar. Painfully shy, with a receding posture that made him look hunchbacked, his mocking sense of humor barely veiled his estrangement from life.

Alfred was his total opposite. The Kafka Studies Department had never had a student like Alfred. He was a magnetic personality who'd parlayed his BA in Germanic Studies into a Fulbright and then a series of business ventures that made him a wealthy man—at least by the standards of the Kafka Studies Department. Where most of the students and faculty were celibate, Alfred had a beautiful Valkyrie of a wife, whom he dressed in exhibitionistically sexy outfits. He made no secret of the fact that he wished his wife to look like one of the prostitutes who hung out at night on the edge of campus and whose services he solicited on his way home from the rare book library.

Martin had everything in common with the men he was studying under. But being self-haters, they were particularly dismissive of him. They preferred Alfred, who was everything they weren't. Martin would come by his advisor's office to hear Alfred's arch voice. He would see Alfred's crossed legs through the half-opened door, an expensive Italian loafer dangling lazily off one of his feet.

Before Martin could even prove himself, Alfred was helping his professors develop a proposal for the National Endowment for the Humanities. He had also fomented a love affair between a beautiful Dostoevsky scholar he'd taken to the track and his mentor, an emaciated looking five-foot five-inch Czech whose PhD was an analysis of Kafka's "A Hunger Artist." Totally ignored in his attempts to get even a modicum of attention, Martin began to founder. When it was time to meet with his advisor, he'd pick up on the distractedness of the man and garble his words. His only paper of the year, an attempt to link the expressionist painting of Edvard Munch to Kafka, had been a self-fulfilling failure. Munch and Kafka had little in common. Everyone knew it was Munch and Strindberg. Yet he couldn't stop himself. The negative attention, the humiliation was more satisfying than a conformity which would have condemned him to live in the shadow of his lusty colleague—whose very life, a series of manipulations, seductions and chicanery, was an affront to everything Kafka stood for.

Then one day, midway in the three-year course, Alfred died. It was that simple. One week he had appeared in class pale and disheveled, the next month he was no more. Apparently Alfred, cocky and confident of his power over life, had ignored the warning signs of the fast spreading cancer that would ultimately kill him. The German word *schadenfreude*, which often appears in the Freudian canon, means the enjoyment of other people's suffering. Such was the hatred Martin had felt that in the final weeks, as life seeped out of Alfred, he allowed himself to thrive as he never had before. It was as if the blood were flowing out of Alfred into Martin. The more the once cherubic wheeler-dealer was diminished by his illness, the stronger, more decisive and more physically imposing Martin became. He learned to stand up straight.

In Alfred's final days, Martin even met a woman with whom he embarked on his first affair. It was as if a huge weight were removed from his shoulders. By the time Alfred died, Martin's fortunes were already on the rise in the department. Within six months Alfred had been all but forgotten and, driven by an almost mystical energy, Martin had been transformed. Where Alfred employed a crude cunning, Martin's energies were characterized by a sense of equanimity and cultivation that far outdid his predecessor. Martin was really putting the Kafka Studies Department on the map and he was winning the attention he had never been able to get before.

The professor who had flunked him on the Munch paper even admitted he might have been hasty. Perhaps there was a connection, he said.

But Martin, having no more need for such futile stretches of the scholarly imagination, politely declined the invitation for a review. No sir! He was interested in power. The way you got it was to play the right hand. Martin was on his way. During this time, he began a romance with Alfred's widow that eventually led to marriage.

One of the items they came across when they were cleaning out Alfred's closet, so Martin could move into the wonderful house Alfred had built, were the very loafers Martin had spotted through the crack in his advisor's office door. Just as his lovely new wife was about to toss them into a plastic garbage bag, he cried "Stop!" He took off the cheap Hush Puppies of the impoverished scholar and tried on one of his deceased rival's cordovans. It fit perfectly.

That same day Martin sat facing his advisor. He laughed to himself, one of the loafers dangling lazily off his foot, as the shadow of the insecure first-year graduate student he had once been approached the half-opened office door.

The Sprinter

One day the sprinter appeared on Rockland Avenue, a hilly winding road off Weaver Street in Larchmont. There were lots of runners on Rockland Avenue. Practically all the families that occupied the split-level, Tudor, or colonial style houses which lined the street had children or adults who ran—sometimes both. But from the first, it was apparent the sprinter was different. He had a chiseled face and grotesquely muscular torso. His forehead was perpetually beaded with sweat from the ferocious workouts he put himself through.

Most everyone knew everyone else on Rockland Avenue, and after the sprinter had shown up every day for a week, neighbors started to ask each other about him.

"Looks like someone training for something," remarked one.

"It's starting to get on my nerves," said another.

It was only when the sprinter's breathing turned into a wheeze as the length of his workouts extended into the evening that some people on Rockland began to think something ought to be done. For weeks on end, rain or shine, the sprinter had not missed a day. He always wore the same tight blue spandex shorts, Golden Wok tee shirt, weightlifter's belt, aerobic shoes, and white tennis headband. There was no variation in his dress or routine, except for the fact that he seemed to be running himself a bit harder each day. And, indeed, every day his frame grew more thin, his jawbone more pronounced, and his eyes more filled with cold determination as he put himself through his grueling paces.

None of those who thought something should be done knew exactly what to do. Though the sprinter's breathing could be heard like clockwork, it could hardly be called disturbing the peace. Everyone was into physical fitness; there were all kinds of bizarre regimens. You couldn't call the police because the sound of someone's jump rope hitting the pavement was bothering you. The *kiais* of karate kickers were as common as the scraping of skateboards. Normally sedate coffee klatches had been replaced by housewives competing against each other on their Peletons. But this was another matter. As autumn passed and the first flurries of winter came, there was no change in the sprinter's behavior.

Only the elderly woman who lived alone at the end of Rockland was heard to comment, "He's the kind of young man who will keep America strong." Indeed, it was an odd form of suicide that masked itself as self-improvement. Day after day, the sprinter seemed to be getting leaner and stronger when, in effect, he was killing himself.

A few residents tried to talk to him. A foot specialist yelled out, "You're hurting your arches!" But the sprinter was unperturbed. As he grew thinner and thinner, wasting away before the eyes of the community, with nobody able to do anything, some folks even began to resent him. Why had he chosen their street for his suicidal mission? At the very least he was a poor example of something—nobody knew exactly what. Narrowness of purpose? Going too far? Overdoing it? No one could seem to find the right words for the behavior which was making the whole neighborhood uncomfortable. It was some state of affairs when you had to keep the blinds shut so your children would not see someone abusing himself outside the window.

Like a car alarm going off in the middle of the night, the sound of the sprinter's breathing was more annoying the more unrelenting it became.

Finally, on New Year's morning, Rockland Avenue awoke to find the sprinter gone. A day passed, then another with no sign of him. Doors would open, then shut. Heads would poke out, looking each way to see if the familiar form was approaching, but there wasn't a sound from him or anyone else in the chill winter air. In the wake of the constant pounding of feet and wheezing, the avenue was engulfed by a deathly silence. Amongst even those residents who had been most unnerved by the sprinter's compulsive behavior, there was a distinct feeling of loss. Everyone had been waiting for life to return to normal, but once it had happened, they felt something was missing. No one would have been unhappy to have the young man back.

People began to wait. But as each day passed, the eerie quietude of winter broken only by the sound of the occasional car engine struggling to turn over in the cold, it became obvious: he was gone for good.

As I
Lay Down

Fred was so devoid of ideas he couldn't get up in the morning. He would sleep until eleven or twelve. When he was finally able to get himself up, he'd drink coffee—as he slowly perused the morning paper—until he couldn't sit still.

Then one morning he awoke from a dream which was the plot of a wonderful short story. It even had a title, "As I Lay Down." His muse had finally spoken. Staring at his clock, which read 6:30, he felt like an enormous burden had been lifted. It couldn't possibly slip through his hands. Not now. He had the whole day ahead, more than enough time to get it all on paper. Finally, his life was about to begin.

Usually Fred wrote down the few ideas he had on the little pad he kept beside his bed. But I don't need to, he thought. I'll be up in a jiffy.

The moments lingering in bed just before getting up were the nicest he had spent in years. Realizing how artful

Staring at his clock ... he felt like an enormous
burden had been lifted from him.

his dream was, he saw himself receiving awards, leading to contracts, fame, and fortune. He was quickly wafted away from the little rent-stabilized studio apartment in the dirty white brick building with its ugly fire escapes blocking the window light. The bed was warm and cozy, the radiator just beginning to clank as the steam came up to heat the chill autumn air. He would just lie in bed with his thoughts a few minutes more, until the nippiness had left the room, luxuriating in anticipation of the smooth path to success that lay ahead. How seldom did he feel this way! There had been times, and each had led to some minor accomplishment. He had never made a killing, but received the kind of small encouragements that whetted his appetite. While laying in bed looking forward to his new life, he fell back to sleep.

When he awoke again, it was noon. He couldn't believe his eyes. If he had only gotten to work right away, he would be so far into "As I Lay Down" that the story would have been a fait accompli. But now, having gotten his usual surfeit of sleep, his head felt heavy. Every time he tried to pick it up, he plunked back down, saying to himself, just five minutes more, I've got my idea. After several bouts of falling back to sleep for five, ten, and fifteen minutes, he awoke with a start. About to reassure himself he had located his ore, he realized he couldn't remember anything more about his story than its title, which itself seemed horribly obvious. "As I Lay Down"…I should have known. It's just what I've been doing, lying down again and again, hoping something will come to me in my sleep, only to awaken to this living death of being a writer without inspiration, without ideas.

Fred began to think his imagination had played a dirty trick on him. Perhaps he was only dreaming when he thought he had gotten up at 6:30 with a wonderful idea. Perhaps his grand idea had only been wish fulfillment—like dreaming a beautiful woman was about to make love to him. His pad was as empty as his bed. That was the proof. There was no story. He didn't know whether to feel relieved he had lost nothing or hopeless about his continuing inability to come up with new ideas.

In his despair he kept falling back to sleep, and by dusk with the setting sun sending the shadow of the fire escape shooting across the floor, the day seemed like one long frustrating dream from which he had yet to awake.

Despite all his attempts to tear it apart as juvenile, he couldn't get the title "As I Lay Down" out of his mind. Scholars are always seeking to discover the lost works of great writers. "As I Lay Down" became his great lost story, the work which would one day redeem him. At the very least, it was a perfect title for the story he was never able to write.

The
Healer

Many years after Frieda stopped seducing the husbands of her best friends, she set out to find the people she had hurt. She would ask their forgiveness and set the slate clean.

She didn't give up the life of the libertine because she wanted to; she gave it up because it was killing her. She would have gone on using her icy good looks forever, if not for her downfall—a series of destructive acts (for instance spraining her ankle while trying to fuck on a fire escape) that became more and more serious. At first it seemed like chance. The bad luck wasn't related to her life. Only with the repetition and severity of the incidents was she forced to concede that something other than accident was involved. And so it was that she sought help.

During her Sexaholics Anonymous rehabilitation, Frieda was discouraged from staying in contact with those she'd acted out with. The time would come, but only when she had recovered from her "soul sickness" and developed a strong spiritual life.

Now that it was her time to go back, she was as anxious to show off her new self as she was to see the old crowd. As she made her first phone calls, she experienced palpitations and began to flush. She was overtaken by the fear that once amongst the friends of the past, she would return to her old ways. After all, she was still sensationally beautiful; her spirituality had only increased her allure. Unlike some converts who became sterile and bland, Frieda naturally gravitated to makeup and nice clothes. And no one discouraged her from enjoying them, if they made her feel better about herself.

However, her fear soon turned to pity. Not only had things gone unchanged for many of her pals, they had essentially gotten worse. The men were flagrant satyrs who insisted on flaunting their infidelities in front of their wives. The women, as surreptitious as ever, would do anything to undermine each other. Everyone wanted to feel power; the sexual antics were too delightful to give up. It was the families who suffered. With each day the quality of peoples' lives got worse. The old thrills were never enough. The acts, justified by some vague notion of ultimate freedom, became ever more egregious and desperate. Frieda, who thought she had seen everything, was appalled. Arriving to visit one or another member of her crew, she came upon scenes of chaos: children running wild and parents drowning their sorrows in alcohol.

Frieda had her work cut out for her. She had come to be absolved. Yet it was obvious more was required. It was her duty to pass on the gift which had saved her life.

It took weeks, months, and in several cases years. Slowly but surely she was making converts. They were her flock, her following. So successful was she in imbuing the principles of her faith that she won over even the most godless and arrogant of the bunch. Now, thriving, ensconced in happy and productive lives, they came back to her for constant guidance. Frieda hadn't set out to be a guru, saint, or prophet. Yet without quite realizing what was happening, she began to enjoy the power.

It had started quite innocently at a dinner party. There was one member of the group who was an iconoclast. He was as devoted to Frieda as any of the others but he liked to challenge her, to play the devil's advocate. She had had enough. The next time they were together she refused to respond when he started up. At first she was hesitant. However, her initial recriminations were followed by rationalization.

"After all," she told herself. "I'm going to feel what I feel."

She ended up making quite a point of it, hugging, kissing, talking animatedly with everyone but him. He wasn't abandoned by the others, though no one came to his defense either. He tried to talk to Frieda about it. Then he tried to talk to those who were closest to her. With the exception of Frieda, who remained stone-faced, everyone was sympathetic, but no one would help. Frieda was entitled. Yes, it was odd that someone so committed to the spiritual life would exclude a suffering person from her graces. Still, Frieda never claimed to be anything other than human. She was entitled to her peccadilloes.

Months passed. The scorned party was displaced by a new object of Frieda's wrath. This time it was a woman, who tried to enlist the support of her predecessor to no avail. After all, why should he? When he had been ostracized, she didn't lift a finger. Now she would have to pay the price. Indeed, she must have done something to have brought this on. And so it continued. The once jubilant get-togethers became permeated by fear as the group waited—like players of Russian roulette— to see who would find themselves at the wrong end of the stick. There was a gruesome pleasure in it.

Rarely an evening with Frieda passed when there wasn't some new drama. Frieda advised a wife, to the exclusion of her husband. She lay her hand on the shoulder of one member of a business partnership while soundly ignoring the other. If you were the victim you suffered; if you weren't, you felt sorry, secretly gloating over the misfortune of others.

As unjust as it all seemed, it was at the same time too delicious to forswear. It was fun vesting power in one person, so long as you were the beneficiary. The small circle became a circle within a circle. There were the haves and the have-nots, those who had access to Frieda and those who did not. The ones who didn't became the untouchables, until such a time as Frieda again acknowledged their existence. There were never any signs or portents; there was no way of knowing how or why Frieda made her judgments. Everyone seemed to be losing something in the process. Lovers were spurned, business relationships collapsed, friends stopped speaking to each other. But it continued unchallenged. The suffering seemed a small price to pay for the exhilaration that came when it was your time to be part of Frieda's court.

The
Book of
Solitude

He had written *The Book of Solitude*, which was really his story. It had become the bible of underground men and women—the mini-Kafkas who live unheralded above the neon-lit bars in New England mill towns, in SROs on the Upper West Side of Manhattan, at the edge of desolate industrial parks, in places like Bayonne. He was swamped by his admirers. At first he opened his heart to them. But then he realized their adulation was tinged with envy, even anger. Where it seemed they admired the man who articulated their wishes and innermost fears, it soon became apparent they felt the story was literally as well as figuratively theirs. It was almost as if they wanted to share the copyright. Feelings of community with his fellow sufferers soon degenerated into claustrophobia. He felt trapped in the little world he inhabited, never having anywhere to go, walking around his tiny Greenwich Village apartment in

He had written "The Book of Solitude,"
which was really his story.

circles, saving the big walk to the deli to buy a bottle of beer for his most desperate moment when he absolutely had to hear the sound of another human voice. Now with people literally camping in front of his door, their eyes beseeching him for attention, he was equally a prisoner. His followers no longer saw themselves in him. He was merely a vehicle for their story. He was the aristocrat, they the angry hordes. Yet he was suffering, suffering even more than before. The success he dreamed would cure his loneliness made nothing different.

Why didn't he move, get an unlisted phone number like so many other celebrities? Was he unwilling to enjoy the fruits of success? Was that the problem? Was his fear of pleasure the reason why he'd become the man he had? He asked himself these very questions, yet it didn't change the condition. He was the man he was. If he refused to modify anything about himself, he wasn't going to be any less lonely. No amount of fame or money would help.

Profit/Loss

They were quite a pair. As he lost weight running, he became even faster, which in turn allowed him to lose even more weight. Her weight training gave her the strength for aerobic workouts, which further increased her strength. Each stride forward led to another, and together there seemed to be no limit to how strong and perfect a couple they could be. The principles by which they improved physically soon infused their working lives. No move was made that was not dictated by necessity. When she went back to law school, she concentrated in the very field—patent law—which would complement his manufacturing business. And, indeed, when she joined a practice, the referrals he gave her, and she him, enhanced their careers. They cross-pollinated perfectly.

It was Monopoly. The idea was to constantly make everything bigger, better, more productive. Once you'd gotten the properties, you populated them with houses, then hotels. Efficiency was the keynote; everything had to produce— everything had to be pushed to its limit. No stone would be left unturned, no opportunity missed. The upward movement of their lives would have continued—soaring off to new heights each day with their morning intake of high protein shakes, low-fat grains and multiple vitamins—had they not been afflicted with the notion they were missing something in not having children.

From the first, their only child, a boy, was trouble. Whether at his pre-school where he refused to make friends with the children of socially prominent parents, tumbling class where he wouldn't join in, or at the dinner table where he preferred a diet of animal fat and ice cream to steamed vegetables, fish, and buckwheat noodles, the child refused to conform. If you looked at a family like you did the profit/loss statement of a conglomerate, the boy was plainly one of the losing segments of the business. For all the strides they had made to become a leaner, more sinuous, intelligent, influential couple, their child grew fatter, more languorous and wasteful as his crucial early years were frittered away.

Instead of "learning toys," he went for silly stuffed animals. In the place of educational videos like *Math Circus*, he chose mindless tapes like *Teenage Mutant Ninja Turtles*. If he had his own way, he would have spent most of his days watching junky cartoons and eating Dipsy Doodles, as opposed to the more appropriate diet of educational TV and seaweed chips his parents prescribed. For a couple who didn't view a movie unless it had historical interest, who saw no purpose in entertainment, their son's addiction to commercial television was just more evidence of the boy's appalling lack of discipline.

The child was sapping them of all their energy, of their very will to live. What was the point of striving when they carried a burden that continually resulted in a zero sum? Their one hope lay in his being a slow starter, a genius like Einstein, who did poorly at first but eventually redeemed himself. He was a costly investment which required repeated infusions of capital to earn back even the money lost. They often expressed the hope he would one day do something so wonderfully productive it would vindicate both him and them in one fell swoop. In reality, they would have been content if he'd simply shown signs of being able to live a normal life of exercise, diet, and education which would contribute to rather than detract from the family's image. If only they could have a child they could be proud of! It was the one dream that always eluded them. Despite all their accomplishments, the little boy, with his rolls of fat, was a rebuke to the svelte, sinewy forms his parents cut.

Pity is a funny thing. Though one of the noblest of emotions, it is only the other side of the coin from disdain. Everyone felt sorry for them; everyone was eager to offer suggestions and advice. But no one was willing to confer any of the rewards they sought. The esteem and adulation they yearned for was reserved for the kind of successful families whose genes everyone envies.

The few hopes they held on to withered as the child fared poorly through grade and high school, ending up to be a living indictment of all parents who have ever had wishes for how they wanted their children to behave. He was like the leak in the dyke which is patched up only to reappear in another place. All progress was diminished by his presence. He was a miscreant, a lump, an excrescence, whose weakness made him all the more difficult to get rid of. While most children were dying to go off into the world, he was content to sit home alone in the tiny maid's room off the kitchen, with its piles of comic books and old portable television, he'd occupied since childhood. The condition only worsened with age. The more they wanted of him, the less he gave. Asking him to contribute simply excited his desire to take. Eventually his parents stopped caring. They let their jobs and their bodies go down the drain, dying heartbroken, a year apart from each other, in their early fifties, despite all the energy they'd put into leading healthy and productive lives.

One day, the son, who was still living alone in the old apartment, woke up with the sun beaming through the windows of the prison he'd created for himself. All of a sudden, he wanted desperately to make up for all the wasted years. He walked out onto the street, breathing in the smell of the new flowers just planted in pots outside his parents' building. Gradually he started working out; he got a job, the first he'd ever had, and went back to school. Unleashed from the wishes and expectations which had been a sorry excuse for love, he began to flourish. It was enough to make any parent proud.

Critical
Mass

They were the type of middle-aged women who were not indisposed to men, but didn't have them and had come to depend upon each other. It wasn't sexual, at least not overtly so. They began to go to concerts and movies and dinners together for want of anything better. Then they became inseparable: two English women living in New York who, having chosen independent lives early on, had nothing to go back to England for. So when they had their falling out, it was a tremendous blow to both. It had been more than a friendship. They were family.

Following the breakup they both decided to escape. They would travel to an exotic far-off place where the disappointments of life could be forgotten. Naturally, being of similar temperament, they chose the same city, Prague, which they loved for its historic Old Town. They were staying in luxury hotels in the same part of town, and it wasn't long before they ran into each other.

Neither would admit it, but the first sight of the other brought instant happiness. The notion of getting away had quickly degenerated for both into a haunting solitude. Rather than feeling freed, being alone in the foreign city had only accentuated their distance from life. Here was a chance to turn things around.

Yet it was a matter of pride. Immediately the smiles with which they greeted each other faded. Each armored herself. With every moment, it became harder and harder to break the ice. Protecting themselves from hurt, they inadvertently made themselves more formidable. If either had been able to be vulnerable, to lose control, the other would have responded. But the dependency was so great—having reached a condition similar to what nuclear physicists call critical mass before the explosive breakup—it was frightening. Besides, they were well-educated Brits whose sense of propriety and grace were lessons they had learned all too well. If nothing else, they knew how to keep up appearances—something that had served them well in their respective careers. Now it had become a trap. The one who spoke up would be acknowledging her need. It was hard enough on familiar ground and near impossible in a strange place where the disorientation made them feel all the more guarded.

As they walked away from each other—having exchanged pleasantries like distant acquaintances rather than friends who knew and loved each other for a quarter of a century—both were filled with recriminations. But the regret at not having done something was quickly followed by a process in which they were able to rationalize the relationship out of existence. *I never really liked her. I never felt close to her.* The thoughts came in a stream. At first it was exhilarating to triumph over the feeling of need. They each felt complete and whole; they couldn't be threatened. The remainder of their vacations were

They would travel to an exotic far off place where they could forget the disappointments of life.

spent walking around the sublime neighborhoods of the venerable old city in increasing solitude. The strength they felt in not giving in was tempered by the realization there was nothing to do but be strong. Before, there had been the hope of getting away. Now that they were away, nothing was improved. They both felt like strangers in life, more desperate than ever, with no outs, nowhere to turn, nothing to look forward to, nowhere to go.

Happily
Ever
After

Even though he was a literary author who steadfastly refused to pander to the multitudes, resigning himself to publication in small magazines, he achieved a major success with a slim novella. The book, brought out by a small press, was picked up by a mass market paperback company and eventually turned into a movie which grossed millions. For quite a time—years, really—he was courted by every agent in Hollywood and editor in New York. There were book deals, magazine assignments, and, of course, script conferences. He stayed at only the best hotels and attended only the most exclusive literary parties.

While he promised himself he would remain true to his convictions, a whole new host of people came into his life—people who were constantly on the move, people he was ashamed to say he preferred over the tired small magazine and press editors with their endless bickering over esoterica. He secretly knew that in order to hang on to this new life, he would have to repeat his success. And as the years went by and it didn't come, he could see his stock declining. He was no longer given a good table at Michael's, nor greeted with the same knowing smile by the maitre d' at Minetta Tavern. It was funny because the work he was producing, the very work the major publishing houses and Hollywood were lukewarm about, was some of his best ever. His old friends at the small magazines and presses would have been delighted to run it. But his agent was vehemently opposed and, while he complained, he basically agreed.

You began to be thought of in a certain way. Yes, it was true that his big success had originally been published by a fine little literary press. But things were different. If a new novel appeared out of the mainstream, after all the years that had gone by, it would surely be perceived as a retreat. There had been some offers from established publishing companies. His agent declined to accept those too. If word got around he'd agreed to a $100,000 advance from Random House, in an age when other well-known writers got $1,000,000, he would be categorized as a mid-list author. So, he wasn't published by the small literary magazines and presses that had made him or the big publishing houses, and soon he even lost the major-league agent who had counseled him to wait.

Panic set in. He belonged neither to the world he had rejected nor to the fast moving one of conglomerate publishing, with its high velocity promotion and big-time money. He was an artist who had inadvertently become an entertainer. Now he was neither. Still, he showed up every day at the little office on 87th Street above the delicatessen where he'd always written. While he told himself he was just writing from the heart, he was really spending most of his time trying to duplicate his early success which had come so naturally. He was like a chemist who creates a magical life-giving elixir and then loses the formula. If someone could tell him how he had done it, he would have gladly repeated himself. When he'd first begun to write, he was proud of his unique vision. Despite the difficulties he had in getting acceptance, he was eager to share it with others. Now, he was less interested in what he wrote than in what would come of it. He desperately needed approval and would do anything to get it. As time went by, he drifted further and further from himself. He was an explorer who has lost his compass. The more he abandoned his early goals, the more confused he became. He didn't know anything anymore. When the work that was the product of this period was ready to be shown, he was sure there would be a host of editors willing to see it. Yet for the first time weeks, even months, passed with no response. When the answers did come, they were all negative. He didn't want to write anymore. He didn't want to do anything. He gave up the small office above the deli. He was receiving royalties from his first and only success, which had become an adolescent classic. They would be enough to enable him to live comfortably for the rest of his life. He moved to a small town in Vermont, where he married the local high school English teacher and lived happily ever after.

Trust

Trust was the name of the game. It was what they had been working on as a couple. It was what would save them from the jealousy and possessiveness by which they trapped each other and themselves. In the name of trust, she went with him to visit the woman who had devastated him, the woman he would have married had he not been left. Now a divorcee with a five-year-old daughter, the woman, he said, was no longer a threat. She was no longer someone he had feelings for—despite the fact he had married his present wife on the rebound.

There were drinks followed by a barbecue. After that, in the atmosphere of trust which was enveloping all three adults, the two old lovers went off to talk in the living room while the man's wife played with his former girlfriend's child in the little girl's room. Even though it made the wife uncomfortable, she believed her husband when he said it was all over. His sole purpose in seeing his old flame was, he said, to understand.

Enough time passed for the little girl to take a nap and wake up again. At first, the wife heard laughter from the dining room. Then there was a long period of silence during which she was sure she heard urgent whisperings and then squeaking, shifting sounds like that of furniture being moved. After forty-five minutes had gone by, her imagination got the better of her. She couldn't take it anymore. She would walk in on them under some pretext. She would say the little girl wanted something to eat or drink, a glass of milk or a cookie. But when she tried to open the door, it wouldn't budge. She immediately assumed the two old lovers had realized breaking up was a mistake. After all, he had talked about how passionate the affair had been. Their marriage hardly compared. It was steady, enduring, full of moments of affection, of attempts to work things out. But there was little of the mystery he described in the other relationship. The atmosphere of trust with its false security was the finale of it all. Now locked out, she felt like a fool. Atmosphere of trust! It was obviously an atmosphere of boredom, full of assurances and lacking in feeling. She hated herself as much as she did him.

She imagined her husband making love to his old flame behind the locked door. She continued to half-heartedly play with the child, at the same time clinging to the little girl as if she were collateral. The child was her security. She would reveal what was going on to the woman's former husband. She would threaten the woman with the loss of her child.

Her thoughts grew in intensity. She was sure they were going to walk in and announce the truth of their relationship. She fantasized the cold determined look on her husband's face. She saw him impenetrable, as she begged him to come back. She saw his courteous, sensitive response merely masking the fact that he cared only for the other woman. She felt small, ugly, powerless. All at once, her husband and his former lover became two outsized romantic creatures adorning the

She had locked herself in.

cover of a paperback romance. As much as she detested the woman, she almost agreed with her husband's choice. There was something right about them. How could she have let this happen? Suddenly, as she tortured herself with alternatingly angry and self-deprecating thoughts, the doorknob turned. When the door wouldn't open, her husband called out to her. There was anxiety in his voice, the alarm of someone worried about a loved one. Looking up, she noticed the children's safety latch had inadvertently been engaged. She had locked herself in.

The
Awakening

His purpose, the thing that gave his life meaning, was the awakening of his torpid wife—a woman who claimed she was uninterested in pleasure, a mere vessel for other people's wishes and desires. She often claimed she never wanted anything, not even him. After being this honest and insistent, she would nervously take back what she said in a half-hearted way that wasn't very believable.

He was tolerant and endlessly hopeful. He devoted his life to making the faulty machine work. He wouldn't give up until he turned his Eliza Doolittle into a desiring, thieving, ambitious human being. He only got angry when she resisted his attempts to change her, asking, "What's wrong with the way I am? So what if I don't want anything? So what if I have no ambitions? Who's to say it's better to be a certain way? What's wrong with the fact that I'd like nothing better than to slump into the armchair and watch TV?" When she made comments like this, he would have angry outbursts. He would threaten to leave, then apologize, and gently try to nudge her "forward" all over again.

She never did the things he wanted. She never embarked on any of the plans he had in mind for her. Money was wasted on therapy, massage, and visualization programs that were never adhered to. But after years of relentless pressure, she finally caved in. She started to do things and, lo and behold, she liked them. It began with one little thing and led to the next. She liked the hands of her masseur. She enjoyed her expensive hairdresser and developed an interest in traveling to the most luxurious resorts. One night she even attacked him in bed, wrestling with him, then starting to "do" him much in the way he had constantly tried to stimulate her. He was shocked and caught off guard. He didn't know how to take it. He felt uncomfortable, but he wanted her to be happy. He didn't dare object to the hedonistic path she was taking for fear it would derail her fragile development. She was definitely changing. There was something strange and frightening about it. Things were happening in a way that was different than he had planned. As she progressed out of her torpor, he was scared he had created a Frankenstein. How else to describe a once prim woman who wouldn't wear a sleeveless blouse now planning a trip to the notorious Club Hedonism in Jamaica? He felt as uncomfortable as she probably had when he was exhibiting his love of life and goading her to join in. However, his exhibitionism, which often consisted of nothing more daring than jumping in a swimming pool, was mild in comparison to someone who couldn't wait to get her clothes off on the nude beach. He wasn't sure he wanted to share the view of his wife's naked body with the world.

Then, during a summer vacation, a long-haired teenager ran by as they walked along a deserted beach.

"He's really good looking," she giggled girlishly.

He had accomplished his task. She had awakened and would leave him. She would choose someone she truly desired rather than simply settling for the man who had presented himself to her. She was no longer a victim who earned things by default. He knew he could explain to her that the light she saw him in was not the only way possible. But he also realized it would be futile. Bitterly, he began to understand that her helplessness had served a purpose; he hadn't been so selfless. What better way to defend himself from the competition of life than to pick a woman who was afraid to make choices. Unfortunately, that was over. She didn't need to wait for him to tell her how she should feel anymore. She was too far gone.

Company History

This family was like the company that is the object of a takeover bid. There were four children. The mother had died of a rare blood disease when the children were small. The mother's family was wealthy. The father, a reserved character who liked nothing better than to sit home reading English murder mysteries and volumes of naval history, found himself gainfully employed by his in-laws. He maintained a legal practice in an elegant art deco building on 57th Street, his in-laws his only clients.

The family lived a modestly affluent existence. There was a pleasant if somewhat inauspicious Park Avenue apartment. All four children attended elite private schools and colleges like Trinity, Andover, Amherst, and Princeton. These, in short, were the assets of the company. The father, it should be noted, was well-connected. An uncle of his had been a famous advisor to the Harrimans—something which gave this particular outfit an extra bit of cachet. The father was not the most demonstrative of men, but he got along with his children. He was especially fond of his youngest daughter, whose interests in history mirrored his own. When she embarked on a career in academia, he encouraged her.

Then one day he saw an advertisement in the *New Yorker* for a cruise to the Galapagos. He would retrace Darwin's journey. On the cruise an older couple took to him. Soon after the boat sailed into New York harbor, they introduced him to their daughter. The woman, a divorcée, who had two sons, turned out to be rich not only due to inheritance, but the generous settlement she had received from her husband. She owned a lavish penthouse apartment and an East Hampton estate.

It was unclear who was about to take over whom. The lawyer found the elegant woman, who turned out to be a psychiatrist, as attractive as she found him. The CEOs were in agreement. If only the employees had felt the same way. What seemed like a friendly merger to the happy couple was looked upon as a hostile takeover by the lawyer's children (the wealthy woman's sons were too young to care). Like executives afraid of losing their jobs when the parent company comes to the fore, the lawyer's children immediately felt rejected by the stepmother, whose icy demeanor and rail-thin figure made her seem more cold than she actually was.

To make matters worse, there was no doubt the children felt uncomfortable with the lifestyle their stepmother represented. Indeed, they rejected her before she ever had a chance to reject them. A stronger woman might have been able to break the barriers of class and style, but for all her abilities and entitlements, she was fundamentally a fragile and defensive creature, who was easily hurt.

If she seemed aloof at the start, she became more so with time, as she defended herself against the divisiveness of her husband's children. The situation was exacerbated by the woman's sons—who were spoiled and had a seductive ability to monopolize their stepfather's attentions.

Though there had been a merger, or takeover, depending on your point of view, the staff of the original company was becoming increasingly estranged. The lawyer's children saw less and less of their father who, for example, now spent Thanksgiving with his wife's parents at their lavish Westchester estate. They came to regard their stepmother as truly wicked and the stepmother regarded them as critical and petulant. She generously invited these strangers into her home, only to find everything she cherished criticized. For all her psychiatric training, she didn't understand the finer points of step-parenting, nor did she care. Her husband's children were old enough to be on their own anyway.

Dissension appeared to be the lot of the subsidiary company, which—though part of a greater whole—acted increasingly like an independent. No sooner did one child get married than he or she was divorced. The divorce of his youngest daughter from an ambitious academic was a blow to the lawyer. Yet he didn't allow it to put him out of sorts. People were always getting divorced these days. Why should his children be any different? For a man of intellect, it was odd that he never mused on the fact that his children's early experience of loss might have something to do with their inability to make relationships work. Within the parent company as well as its subsidiary there existed a huge trove of intelligence that wasn't put in the service of memory. It was as if the computer managing all the operations was constantly breaking down. Information was not being processed correctly.

Then the lawyer was diagnosed with colon cancer and died. It all occurred very quickly, before anyone had a chance to realize what was happening. The *coup de grace* came at the funeral where the lawyer's son gave the eulogy. He managed to discuss everything he could about his father's career, his schooling, his friends, without so much as mentioning the wife. It was the final act of revenge. The mother, sitting with her two sons in the front pew, walked out without saying a word to her stepchildren. In fact, they never spoke again. All matters pertaining to the estate were handled through their attorneys.

At last the lawyer's children were free. The employees had bought back the company. But independence is purchased at a price. After the negative experience of the takeover, it was hard to trust anyone. They had achieved self-determination. However, they were sorely in need of precisely the kind of direction they were no longer able to accept.

So their world became smaller. They relied on each other, but were unable to reach out to each other in ways that could perpetuate family unity. Rather than becoming a source of strength, they sapped each other's energy. The company was in the red. Like a bankrupt firm that sells its final assets, the four impelled back into life by the untenability of their existences, all married and divorced again and again. Occasionally they would get together. Yet it was nothing like their upbringing when they were four children who proudly stuck together, in the face of an early and tragic loss.

The
Night
Man

He knew more about her than her mother and father ever had and certainly more than her husbands and lovers. He had known her from the moment she was carried home from the hospital, through her adolescent years sneaking boys up when her parents were away. After her parents died and her marriage fell apart, she moved back into the apartment.

Being the night man was a lonely occupation. It was just Joe working both elevators and the front door. She never said much, yet the intimacy of knowing her secrets held out a hope. It wasn't as if he expected consummation. She treated him no differently than the family schnauzer, an undemanding presence she could be comforted by and indifferent to at the same time. However, he came to feel close to her, thinking his knowing so much would somehow come to something, somehow provide a conclusion, lend a meaning to the tedious succession of solitary nights. Or was it the need to find meaning that started him thinking about Missy the way he did? Yes, it had to amount to something. Isn't that an emotion we all feel? Despite all the evidence to the contrary, don't we all expect the years—in which we've waited for this or that to begin or end—to culminate in something other than feebleness and death?

Joe retired on his sixty-fifth birthday. He would have continued. He had never married; he didn't like to drink. He had nowhere to go. He was losing his teeth and there is something comforting about the big old lobby of a Park Avenue apartment house when you can't chew. But the building was strict about retirement. He didn't have a choice.

Joe didn't think about it until the moment his last shift ended. It was only on his way out with the black lunch box and the thermos that held his milky tea that he realized he wouldn't see Missy anymore. It was as if he suddenly had been covered with his own burial shroud. He kept on walking, but he felt dead. He stared back at the gold trim of the canopy. A few tenants had wished him well. He was given several cards, even some money. Yet when Missy came in the night before there wasn't even a "Good-bye, Joe."

"Probably has something on her mind," he thought.

He wouldn't have dared say anything to her. He took pride in what he did. Even when a tenant came in tipsy and said a lot of things, he took special care to keep his head bent the next day, as if nothing had happened. He slowly closed the door behind her that last time he saw her, as she fumbled for her keys. He could hear her say "damn." Then there was the clicking of her heels as she walked across the marble lobby floor to the A/B line elevator. That was the last he ever heard from Missy.

Being the night man was a lonely occupation.

Collectors

Experience was something you photographed. The Channings had almost every moment of their children's lives on film. The first smile, the first steps, the first meal of real food—all these experiences were saved for posterity. Unfortunately, Barbara and Bill Channing were so eager to capture experiences, like lepidopterists' rare butterflies, they seldom actually lived these moments. They prided themselves in their mastery of old-fashioned photography. The focus, the f-stop, and the shutter were their concerns. Then there were the negatives, the prints, the enlargements, and the reproduction antique photo albums, all exactly alike, lined up on a shelf of the living room bookcase. Bill and Barbara never looked at their photographs. They kept saying they were going to. But there were too many. The more the pictures piled up, the more they put off looking at them. They collected snapshots the way people hoard money. Sometimes Bill Channing would stare proudly at the tomes. It was wonderful having a wife and children, he thought, running his hand along the spines that grew along the wall like the shell of an oyster covering some marvelous pearl.

Then one day they returned from a vacation in Jamaica to find a ceiling leak had ruined the collection. The heavy gray album paper had so effectively absorbed the massive outpouring of water from the upstairs neighbor's faulty radiator valve that the images had been destroyed. The sacrifice they had made—in giving up the spontaneous experience of their children in order to preserve it—had come to naught. Now they had nothing, neither memories beyond a series of camera bags, flash attachments, and boxes of film, nor the photos themselves.

The destruction of the albums was very much like a bank failure during the Depression. Their savings were wiped out. The childhoods of their two children were now irretrievable. True, they had a smattering of digitalized images on their computer, but this was a small consolation.

Barbara spirited the children off to bed while Bill surveyed the damage. When she returned, she was shocked to find Bill exposing the undeveloped film from their trip.

"What are you doing?" she screamed.

Bill danced around the room, waving the exposed rolls in the air and letting them unravel like streamers. At first Barbara was frightened. Had Bill been traumatized? Had he lost his mind? Then she started to laugh. Grabbing a roll of 35mm Color 400 marked "Ocho Rios," she unwound it and followed him.

They never took another picture of their family again. But from that day on, they were blessed with wonderful memories of their children.

Imagination

The harried wife and three small children were a burden. Kogin devoted most of his time to his fledgling brokerage business, which was always on the point of collapse. They bought a suburban house they couldn't afford. He never had any money. While his wife dreamed of security, he thought only of escape. To make enough to escape the woman who had been his high school sweetheart. To escape his children. With the exception of a few flings, he had never really known other women. For that matter, he didn't know his children—three screaming creatures who swarmed around him like flies when he returned from work. After an uncomfortable ride in a crowded Long Island Railroad car, he was tired and irritable. Like insects, he shooed his children away. Once the children were in bed, they would eat dinner in silence. Then he would go to the garage, where he puttered with parts for his boat. The evening would end with his wife complaining about how apathetic he was toward her. Sometimes there would be a fight. More often, by the time he was ready to get into bed, she would be sound asleep. Caring for three small children all day was work.

One day while out on the Long Island Sound, Kogin fell out of his boat. The helm was in a position that made the boat travel in a circle. It started back at him and suddenly his arm was sliced by the propeller when he ducked under to avoid the bow. He felt no pain in his arm, but was unable to move it. He was floating in the middle of the Sound, bleeding to death, with an arm he would later learn was almost completely severed from his shoulder. All at once he realized he might never see his family again and he understood how much they meant to him. They say at the moment of death you see your whole life flashing before your eyes. That's what happened to Kogin. Only he lived. He was picked up by a passing speedboat, which appeared to him as a dot on the horizon. He was rushed to Northshore Hospital in time to save the arm.

It was a bad dream and he had awakened in the prime of his life. Most men who have had trouble being fathers feel remorse when it's too late. By then their children despise them. But his relationship to his wife and children was young enough to be repaired. Even though he was an eccentric character, as finicky about food (he only ate hamburgers) as he was about people (he didn't like them), he became a devoted father and husband. Just at the point when he no longer cared about making a fortune, he became an enormous success. This is just one of those very happy stories. There isn't much else to tell.

Radio

As a child, Spector was left alone when his parents went out at night. Once, he got in his parents' bed, where he slept until they came home. He was afraid to leave because of all the strange shadows and reflections. The inlaid faces on a pair of oriental living-room lamps became a particularly ghastly apparition in the semi-darkness. As the evening progressed, Spector's imagination made the shadows into creatures which would leap out at him, were he to cross the threshold out of the bedroom.

The irony was the one thing that allowed him to go to sleep—the voices from the maroon Zenith radio which sat under his mother's night table—were the source of harrowing nightmares. There was nothing worse than awakening from a nightmare after one of these broadcasts. Everything was heightened. The rest of the apartment was like an Amazonian rain forest, abuzz with terrifying sounds. And when he awoke—at one or two in the morning—the radio stations at that time, the 1950s, would already be off the air. Only static would be coming through the receiver. The lively, comforting voice of the announcer was gone.

The voices from the maroon Zenith radio were
the source of harrowing nightmares.

Naturally, his parents, great party-goers that they were, would be nowhere near coming home.

Usually he fell asleep to *Sea Hunt*. He saw himself going down to the ocean bottom, as the sound of aqualung bubbles was interrupted by a commercial. His fourth grade class had gone on a trip to the NBC radio studios in Rockefeller Center; they visited the sound effects room where thunder was produced by hitting a huge sheet of metal with a mallet. But when his imagination took over, it all became terribly real. The descent into sleep was literally accompanied by the sound of oxygen escaping into the sea. Waking up from his dream, in a sweat, he'd have to reassure himself he wasn't on the ocean floor. He prayed for his parents finally to return home. How he welcomed the sounds of the elevator door opening and his father's key in the lock. His mother would lean over to kiss him, then his father would carry him back to his own room. During the winter months, after he'd been out playing in the snow, he would enjoy the relief of the hot water running over his feet in the tub. This was how he felt when his parents finally got home. All the fear was worth the warming security of their presence. Suddenly nothing was frightening. By the next day, he'd be ready to accept another two dollars from his mother (the fee she paid him to babysit for himself), before the terror began. For years the succession of night terror and relief defined his life.

Then, reaching adolescence and going away to college in the golden age of television, his fear of the dark wore off. The private world he created out of the voices of radio actors and sound effects was hidden away in a corner of his mind. The face of Lloyd Bridges replaced the image he'd conjured of the intrepid underwater troubleshooter. There was a real Lone Ranger, a real Hopalong Cassidy. Actual horses' hooves—not the odd wood blocks they'd seen in the NBC radio studio—produced the sound of galloping.

However, though he had repressed them, the haunting images were never far away. One spring evening, coming home to find a note from his wife saying she had left with the children, the nightmares returned. They were horrible nightmares in which he crossed the threshold of his parents' bedroom to find himself engulfed in darkness. In one, he was back in the old apartment (which had been sold shortly after his parents' death), totally lost, unable to negotiate his way back to the safety of the bedroom. He walked into a closet thinking it a hallway or down a corridor leading away from instead of towards light. It was like a *Sea Hunt* episode where oxygen deprivation made it hard to tell up from down. Thinking he was saving himself, he was swimming frantically to his death.

Spector's heart was pounding when he woke up. He couldn't run to his father's bed for comfort. There was no father, or wife for that matter. He was alone, afraid to go back to sleep, afraid of the darkness that was enveloping him.

The
Young
Wife

Lisbeth, his father's young wife, was cultivated. His crass and uncouth father had married his opposite. Spector felt it his prerogative, indeed his duty, to play the role of confidant. He would be someone his father's bride could talk to.

When his father and stepmother were in the heat of their passion, Spector's mother was sitting in the dark den of their apartment watching movies about tragic romance like *Intermezzo* and *Brief Encounter* with her impressionable son. In contrast, his stepmother was his age. If his father hadn't already snagged her for himself, she was someone Spector could easily have brought home. Would his father have tried to steal her away, as he himself was now doing?

Every night when his father got home, Spector and Lisbeth would be drinking together in the den. Chatting up authors and books he had never even heard of, his father eyed the pair suspiciously. But it was also gratifying having his son, so disdainful of his success as a businessman, enamored of something he possessed. And it was nice Lisbeth and Spector got along. Spector not only entertained Lisbeth, he also reflected positively on the man who'd engendered him. And it was uncanny how much Lisbeth and Spector had in common: their love of Woody Allen films, Anita Brookner novels, and the exotic Caribbean island of Mustique. It was as if they were friends in some former life from which the father had been excluded.

The one running joke between Spector and his mother had been his father's bombast. They shared a mocking humor based on an unspoken set of assumptions about the nature of things; it was at the heart of the love they felt for each other. Watching his father negotiating with a maitre d' over where they were being seated, Spector would smirk knowingly at his mother. There was nothing they could do about him. Of course, for someone who didn't know how to handle himself, Spector's father had done pretty well in life. Spector had never been able to earn a cent.

Spector's father had been a prodigy—a young man on the rise—when his mother first met him. She had seen something in him. But Lisbeth was no different than Spector, who regarded the old man as a vulgar, overbearing oaf. Plainly she was using him. Though Spector coveted her, he felt sorry for his father and himself. Even if she drank and flirted with Spector, she would replace him the minute she inherited his father's fortune. It was the first time he and his father had the same enemy. They were both losing out. Yet there was no way he could say it. His father, highly sensitive and insecure, would react violently if Spector told him the woman he was passionate about was making a fool of him.

Oh yes, Lisbeth was having her fun. She seemed smug and self-satisfied in the knowledge everything was going well for her. She even liked to egg Spector on as he leveled his attacks at the old man. It was to her benefit. Let those two hate each other to death. That would ensure her inheritance. She was getting away with murder. At first it had been so lovely, so right. Now he realized the love he felt for his father's new wife was only tying the noose around his own neck. With the fortune she'd inherit, she could have a thousand young men just like him.

The lifestyle of the rich man's son had been the one consolation for his miserably unfulfilled life. The young wife was no more than the agent of his impoverishment. He began to stay away from the apartment. He couldn't bear to look at her. As he avoided the cocktail hours and dinners, the newlyweds were left alone. He gloated with satisfaction as he saw his father's relationship with his beautiful bride fall apart.

Breasts

The first night Spector slept with Molly, the night they met, he fell madly in love with her breasts. They were perfect breasts. If it can be said that every human being—male or female—has some idealized vision of the breast, representing everything they once had or didn't have as an infant, then these breasts epitomized the ideal that had always eluded him.

To describe the exact shape and size of Molly's breasts would hardly do justice to Spector's feelings. After all, there are lots of breasts big and small, with light little nipples or large dark areolae. There are even breasts with hair and men who love them. Suffice it to say that Molly's breasts were on the small side, perfectly upright, roughly the size of tennis balls.

While everyone is attracted to one kind of breast or another, few base their feelings on this factor alone. But Molly's were like Cinderella's slippers. They so perfectly fit Spector's idealized image, he couldn't stop fondling them. Spector had never behaved so manically. The sight of her breasts ignited a force that reached to the depths of his being.

As he left her small brownstone apartment after their initial evening together, he felt like he was dying a little. She gave him a queer look when he couldn't resist one last squeeze.

It was three days before he saw Molly again. Spector was in torment. In fact, he was unhappy any time he couldn't be near her two wonderful breasts. The problem was, Molly's breasts were the only thing Spector liked about her.

Lucky for Spector, Molly was head-over-heels in love with him from the start. His inability to keep his hands off her breasts in the Japanese restaurant he took her to that second night was annoying, as was his manic fondling before and after sex, but she put up with it, not wanting to rock the boat.

On their third date, realizing what a dope she was, Spector almost got up from the table during dinner. It was his chance to save himself. When they got back to her place, she let him unfasten her bra. At the sight of her beautiful breasts, he fell to his knees and proposed marriage.

Rather than becoming bored with her breasts, once Molly moved in with him and he could see them every night, he became more obsessive. He couldn't get enough. He needed to touch them more and more. If in the beginning her perpetual whining had been a problem, he no longer thought twice about it. Saying he needed to talk, he would invite her downtown for lunch. They always met in the same darkened rear booth of a deli on 40th Street. They sat facing the wall so he could stick his hand up her shirt. Molly was the kind of woman who was able to oblige an obsession without feeling she was doing anything out of the ordinary. For instance, when she met Spector for lunch she instinctively knew to wear blouses that buttoned down the front, but she never would have admitted either the necessity of it or the abnormality of the situation. Her unconscious did the work. She was able to palliate her husband without recognizing something was wrong.

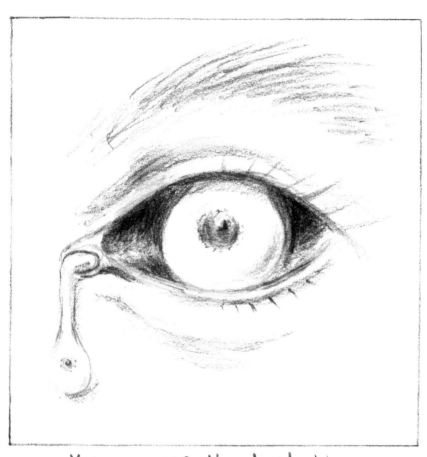

Majorca was the last time
Spector ever touched Mollie's breasts.

Then one day in the middle of a vacation to Majorca, Spector and Molly went swimming on the local beach where virtually all the women were topless. It was an extremely hot afternoon. Spector fell asleep, awakening in a groggy stupor. Wiping his eyes and staring out at the water—which seemed like a mirage—he immediately spotted a fleshy form rolling out of control in a large wave. Standing up, his eyes immediately fixated on the breasts, as the woman he thought to be Molly was thrown onto the shore. They seemed rounder, more beautiful than ever. Driven by his characteristic tunnel vision, he ran behind her and cupped a hand around each breast, convinced he was comforting the shivering form of Molly. Imagine the horror he felt when the woman turned, screamed, and slapped him squarely across the face.

Molly, who herself had been coming out of the water, couldn't believe her eyes. It was as if all the suspicions she had repressed came to the surface at once. When Spector reached out to touch his drug, his lifeline—her breasts—she slapped him too. She slapped him again and again, until exhausted, she fell to the ground, bursting into tears.

Majorca was the last time Spector ever touched Molly's breasts. She moved into a separate room at their hotel and requested a divorce as soon as they returned to New York.

Falling
Body

He heard a branch snap, then a cracking sound. It all happened so fast he could do little more than get out of the way. But afterward he would tell someone the sound of the woman falling to the pavement from the hotel was that of a flower pot breaking. When he turned around he saw the body, lying in a puddle of blood and, at her side, the branch the woman took with her as she descended. Had she grabbed at it in a last desperate attempt to live, or was dead weight simply destroying whatever was in its way?

Already there were sirens. Before he knew it, two paramedics tightened the belts of a body bag as a detective threw the woman's scattered sandal in with the remains. It was the kind of beaten-up old thing used around the house as a slipper. Had she purchased it in happier days on some sunny Greek island? It had been a sad foreshadowing of the crumpled corpse. The broken branch, the blood stained pavement, the jaded policemen keeping back the carnival crowd—it all spoke for the moment life has been taken away.

Spector wanted the policemen to shut up. Their constant banter was distracting from something that was at once brave, cowardly, and awesome. You could feel the finality of the woman's decision as you looked at the mess on the sidewalk. The Pakistani newsstand dealer's window looked out over the scene of death. Throughout it all business had gone on as usual. Spector walked away as two ambulance drivers began to argue about how to back out without hitting a double-parked car.

For several days after, Spector scanned the *Times*, the *Post*, the *News*. Surely a woman jumping from the Gramercy Park Hotel would merit an article, at the very least a mention along with the murders, robberies, and rapes reported in "metropolitan news." He studied the obituaries. Nowhere was the woman's death recorded. Was it so common for people to jump from buildings? Was the city raining bodies? The rest of the world was going on with their business. Yet he couldn't get the woman out of his mind—a woman he didn't know, whose body had fallen in his way.

He saw himself walking across Third Avenue before it happened. If he'd simply turned the corner and gone to the deli or ducked into the adult section of the local news store where he was constantly tempted by the lurid covers, he wouldn't have been plagued by the memory. But the moment was dead. He wished he could go back to it, as if it were something tangible, as if it were still alive. If only life were like a video that could be rewound. The images of the street, of himself walking, of the woman perched on the window ledge or roof—every second was evanescent, as dead as the instant a falling body hits the ground.

A
Splendid
Dish

The only way out—killing her—was unoriginal. How many stories had he read in those Alfred Hitchcock compilations where a husband or wife does away with the partner they can't divorce? He'd get caught. Still, he was too guilty to leave her. That was out of the question. He simply couldn't face it.

Yet day by day, he hated everything about her—the way she walked, the way she talked, the dresses she wore. She was shrinking before his eyes. Once an attractive woman, with a classic WASPy face, she'd grown drawn and pale, her stare glazed and hollow. The enormous rings under her eyes made her look like an apparition at a séance, a visitor from the world of the dead. If he simply kept thinking his horrible thoughts, he wouldn't have to do anything. She was already as thin as a rail. One morning he would awaken to find a corpse next to him in bed. It was just a matter of time.

Then one evening as they sat silently at dinner, she popped out with: "Richard Mayer called. We're going to do some museums tomorrow afternoon."

Mayer was the English banker she'd been seeing when Spector swept her off her feet.

"The Jew," Spector mused dismissively.

What did it matter to him? Mayer, enormously wealthy, lived on an estate. Caroline had given it all up to live in the dank little Gramercy Park studio with the man she loved.

"Fool," Spector thought.

When they were first going out, there had been some horrible scenes as Mayer fought for a place in Caroline's life.

"Me or him, you have to choose," was the ultimatum Spector leveled at her.

She had made her choice. Spector's domineering personality had descended over her like a dark cloud; she couldn't escape it. Back then, she didn't even want to.

Over the years Mayer had kept in touch. He called whenever he was in the States on business and even though Spector berated her for it—"You like that weakling just for his money and you know it," he would say—she never let go.

It was a programmed response. Spector was about to get angry at her again, when he stopped.

"Let her have her fun," he thought, "she doesn't have much time left anyway."

Mayer would take her to Daniel and Bemelmans Bar at the Carlyle—the places Caroline loved which Spector could scarcely afford. Rather than feeling jealous and competitive as he had in the past, he felt grateful to Mayer for making him magnanimous. The once possessive husband was letting his wife do what she wanted. It would be a lovely send-off.

The road to hell is paved with good intentions.

Spector laughed mockingly at the catchphrase.

The next morning, as he leaned down to give Caroline the perfunctory goodbye kiss, she grabbed him, holding his head against her breast. He hated her smell, he detested her sallow skin. She was like a drowning person pulling him under. Unable to control his disgust, he wrenched himself away. Usually Spector went through the motions. Now the hatred was so obvious, Caroline was shocked.

"I have a kink in my neck," he lied.

That evening when Spector returned from work, Caroline came to the door in a new dress. Her faded blonde hair had been frosted. Her skin was rosy and fragrant. Miraculously, she had returned to her former self.

The dinner table was elegantly laid, the candles lit. Suddenly, Spector was filled with delight. As he watched Caroline walking to the kitchen, he fell back in love. Looking at her, he experienced the exact opposite of the syndrome he had experienced before; the more positive he felt about her, the more beautiful she became. Something in him wanted to stop it. If he could only have the old thoughts, he would free himself from this dying soul once and for all. But the power of the life force is unstoppable. His good feelings and her lovely appearance were an unbeatable combination. He felt more and more warmly towards her with each passing minute and she, in turn, looked better and better. If he couldn't consummate his desire shortly, he would burst.

As he walked out of the kitchen towards the bedroom where he would surprise her, he caught sight of two well-polished black oxfords. Looking up, he saw Mayer in his double-breasted pinstriped suit, his hair slicked back, champagne glass in hand. Turning, he met Caroline's stare. The hollowness was gone from her eyes. A piercing determination had replaced her glazed look.

"Richard is staying."

The words were a double blow, since at the very moment she spoke them, he realized the table was set for two.

She took a barbecue fork from the counter and stabbed it into the duck that sizzled in a roasting pan atop the stove. She placed the bird on a platter and proudly carried it to the table. Crisply roasted, browned all over, it was a splendid dish.

Crisply roasted, browned all over,
it was a splendid dish.

The

Heavy

Spector couldn't believe it. After leaving several messages on his friend's answering machine and getting no response, he called him at his office. The voice was so hesitant and unfriendly Spector barely recognized it.

"I'm on another line," the friend said petulantly. "Can I call you back?"

He never did. Only two months before, Spector had been invited to the friend's wedding. He couldn't go. Was that the reason for the coldness? Or was it something that had been brewing? Did his failure to attend merely provide the final excuse for the break? If his failure to attend the wedding was just an excuse, was it something Spector had done before? Or did it have nothing to do with him? If it was something he had done, theoretically there was something he could do to undo it. A thousand possibilities crossed his mind. But finally he decided he'd gone far enough. He had done nothing wrong. If his friend had been offended by something Spector wasn't aware of, it could not have conceivably been egregious enough to warrant the response.

A year passed. Spector thought about his friend all the time. But he remained resolute about not doing anything more until his friend made a gesture. Then one day while walking across 23rd Street, Spector spotted his friend coming towards him, plugged into his earbuds, staring at the ground. Spector was sure the friend had seen him. He could have played the same game, turning his head away, outdoing his friend at his own game. But something made him run over to the friend whose involuntary smile soon turned to a look of scorn, as the thoughts—whatever they were—returned.

"I think about you all the time," Spector offered expansively. "I'm not happy about the situation. Sometimes it's good to talk about these things."

"When it's time," the friend said sternly.

Still more years passed. The friend never became ready. Perhaps if Spector had done something provocative, it might have justified a conversation, but more likely than not what was embarrassing to the friend was that it wasn't anything specific. There weren't any reasons for the disaffection, other than a generalized loss of interest which was too difficult to explain. Yet, even as Spector's new life grew around him, he couldn't get the unanswered question of why the friend summarily broke off their relationship. *I've done something. I must have done something. But I didn't do anything.* He couldn't stop the constant dialogue in his head. Sometimes he was furious with his friend for not freeing him from the mystery. At other times, he was understanding, apologetic, and even willing to accept blame. Anything to get a conversation going.

Finally one day, almost ten years later, Spector decided he couldn't bear living out the rest of his life with the ache of not knowing what had destroyed the friendship. He picked up the phone. His friend was the kind of person who screened calls. He expected to be sent to voice mail, but his friend picked up right away. The friend was delighted to hear from Spector. Again Spector was uncomprehending. What had happened?

It was several weeks later when they met that Spector learned his friend was suffering from a chronic neurological disorder. The friend seemed to have some notion of the fact something had happened. However, there was no sense of the enormous period of time that had passed and no remembrance of the reason why the friendship had ended. His friend had aged terribly. He was beginning the decline into the kind of sickly old age where a once independent being becomes reduced to behaving like a helpless child.

"What are you doing next week?" his friend asked, just before they parted.

"Why?"

"I thought we might go to the movies."

Spector was angry. He hadn't come to be friends. The friendship was long over. He'd come to find answers. Now he was turning out to be the heavy. How unfair life was.

Sleep

All at once Spector was living the kind of life he'd dreamed of. When the chairman of the company who had promoted him from a lowly sales position to president in a year said "jump," he did. Gone were the questioning and hesitancy. Gone was the insistent individuality. Suddenly he was traveling in a circle that assumed a familiarity with the latest products, foods, inventories, and inventions. When he went for outings on the chairman's yacht, most of the scantily clad young women were tinkering with one or another piece of gadgetry—either the newest Apple Watch or iPhone. One woman was able to receive emails on her wrist. She had run an incredibly successful chain of bakeries and was reputedly responsible for introducing real bagels to the Midwest.

It wasn't a question of Spector declaring his identity—whatever that was. No one paid any attention to you unless you possessed certain things, which functioned as passwords. Not only did you have to have them, you had to make it appear as if you had always had them, as if you had always lived the kind of life where people traveled to Dubai and Petra in the company of expensive luggage and laptops. It was work for a lonely recluse whose pleasure had come in showing how much he didn't want the things others did, who only a year before had spent the greater part of his weekends sleeping. But Spector did more than succeed. He triumphed.

When Spector was invited on the chairman's yacht, he searched far and wide for the latest device no one had heard of—a thimble-sized object that projected NFTs on the wall. Nonchalantly prancing up the gangplank with it, he became the life of the party. After years of solitude, Spector had a girlfriend. He was in love, but he was afraid to let her get close for fear she would discover the truth about him. He didn't know what he was going to do. Someday she would find out that he was not nearly as sophisticated, easygoing, and lighthearted as he made himself out to be. If she discovered the pettiness, fear, and discomfort at the heart of his being, she would surely leave him. Anyway, he was starting to enjoy his new self. Even though he was becoming the kind of happy-go-lucky person he had always envied and hated, he was beginning to feel okay for the first time. It was a curious feeling that he was afraid of losing—so much so that his fondest wish was that he could erase his past, pretend it didn't exist. He had everything he wanted: a woman who made heads turn, a prestigious job, and a classy car.

"You really ought to get one of these," his boss had said, as they buzzed from the helicopter to the yacht one afternoon.

The next day Spector was the proud possessor of a self-driving Tesla.

It felt so good. There were a constant stream of people and parties. Everyone knew him. How different this was from his first marriage, when his wife and he walked miserably around New York on summer weekends with nothing to do, hating themselves and blaming each other for their plight.

The thing he dreaded the most was running into anyone from his old life who might laugh at his clothes, haughty behavior, or car. It would be so humiliating; he was having nightmares about being discovered, about having it all taken away. If only he could no longer be the son of his parents, no longer the ex-husband of his ex-wife, then the chain would be broken. He would be free to be what he wanted.

The deep afternoon sleeps of the kind Spector had fallen into were the most painful to wake from, especially when, as now, he opened his eyes in darkness, unable to orient himself. He was lying on the bare mattress, the sole furnishing his wife had left him when she moved out. He took a sip of warm beer from an open bottle which sat by his side. It was always the same dream, beginning on Saturday and continuing on and off for the rest of the weekend. His sleep was becoming deeper and deeper. It was increasingly difficult to get himself up. As much as he wanted to die, to end the despair of his solitary life, he feared the dreams in which he slowly drowned. Maybe he would accomplish his goal. Maybe he could eradicate his old self. Maybe he wouldn't wake up.

Out of Sight,
Out of Mind

Spector had always hated the kind of men who flirt with women in front of their own wives. The poor creatures cower uncomfortably between outrage and competitiveness—usually choosing the latter in a futile attempt to win back what they have already lost (or perhaps never had). However, his secretive afternoon trysts with a young waitress were driving him mad in another way, that was less sadistic, but more profoundly threatening. Though they lasted only an hour in her Columbus Avenue walk-up, they occupied his consciousness for most of his day. Sitting cross-legged opposite his wife at the tatami table of their favorite Japanese restaurant, as she gazed out serenely, he felt like the biggest liar, thief, and cheat who had ever lived. He couldn't go on with the deceit. In addition, despite the passion he felt, he knew he was exploiting the perverse attraction of a young woman who only liked unavailable men. He would never know the waitress, nor she him. Their images of each other were the stuff of fantasy—created out of a relationship which could only live as long as it was ephemeral. Theirs was an affair predicated on impossibility. She would lose interest the minute he left his wife, the minute the relationship became a reality. And he knew intellectually the same could be said of him.

Of course, he could have left his marriage for a sequence of these fleeting romances with younger women. This way he could effectively insulate himself from the whines, groans, and wrinkles of age. Nubile waitresses working nights to finance hopeless acting careers. Supple, ageless bodies, one after the other. That could have been his out. But he would never get close to anyone, nor would anyone ever get close to him. The fantasy of total escape filled him with a loneliness, more tormenting than mortality itself.

No, he wasn't ready to change anything. At the same time, he knew he couldn't go on the way he was, constantly acting, dishonest, estranged from himself. Slowly, gently, he would let his wife know what was occurring. He would drop subtle hints, in bits and pieces, the way he administered medicine to their children when they were young, giving a drop or two, followed by a mint, then another drop until the appropriate dose had been furnished.

After months of this, Spector felt he had accomplished his task. His appointment calendar had been left open. Little notes from his lover lay on his desk. His lover's perfumy smell lingered on his body. He felt he had gradually let out the truth, without hurting his wife. What did she think? Probably nothing. It was an affront she let rest below the surface of her consciousness. Oh, if it came to it, she might admit: My husband is having an affair with a younger woman. But what man doesn't sow his oats? At least he's loyal and loving, she reasoned. Her self-sacrifice was worth it. He was proud of himself. He had done it. He felt whole again.

It was a hot day at the end of August. The affair with the young waitress was at its peak, as torrid as the unrelenting heatwave that had hit the city. Her apartment only had a weak ceiling fan. They rolled around in their sweat until he fell off her, speechless, exhausted, gazing at her naked body curled up on the bed, still wanting her as a crack of hall light crept into her darkened studio. Then he stumbled out into the hot afternoon sun as she slept soundly.

Spector knew he had to get away, and suggested a trip to the beach to his wife. Having arrived, he stared out at the waves, thinking only of his mistress, as his wife walked towards him, pulling off her old-fashioned swimming cap and shaking the water from her arms and legs.

"That was great," she said. "Why don't you take a dip, dear?"

All things considered, it had been a lovely weekend. Both their children were away, one in Europe, the other in his final year of sleep-away camp. They were staying in the modest motel outside Montauk—where they had once gone on weekends, when the kids were young.

There were even some romantic moments as they walked along the beach at sunset, recalling the times they'd gone hunting for rocks and shells with their oldest son—then five—as they cradled the younger one in their arms. He didn't feel the kind of passion for his wife that he felt for the waitress, but he experienced a closeness, the first closeness they'd had in years. After they made love, she fell asleep on his chest, just the way she did when they were graduate students having an affair twenty-five years before. That had been the big secret then. But it had been a lovely secret, something they decided to keep from their colleagues in the small Kafka

He was staring out at the waves
thinking only of his mistress.

Studies Department, for professional reasons. When they were ready to get married, they would tell. The conspiratorial nature of the undertaking gave the affair an extra added thrill. It made it luscious. Spector felt proud, in control, instead of shameful and dirty the way he recently had. We've been so close, he thought, and she knows all about it. She won't mind if I confide in her. It will be our little secret, just like the other one once was. Perhaps it will even bring us closer together. There's nothing like honesty.

As he proceeded to tell the truth, he thought of his wife one night early in the relationship, lying in bed after making love, her legs pulled up against her chest as she shared a peccadillo of her fantasy life. She'd felt trusting and had laid herself bare.

Spector's plan didn't work out as expected. His wife hadn't gotten any of the hints. If anything, she had defended herself ever more fiercely from what she didn't want to know—by refusing to pay attention to the evidence he put before her eyes. The warm sun of an idyllic afternoon became the baking light of the interrogator's lamp. Frozen in place by her steely glare, he didn't so much as dare to get up to put lotion on or move into the shade. She questioned him unrelentingly.

Who was she? How long had it been going on? Where did they meet? How was it? And yes, what exactly did they do? He knew she meant business. Frightened, he answered all her questions without protest. By the time she was done with him, he was red as a beet. The hours sitting in the sun without moving had resulted in a terrible burn. He was in the twilight of his middle years, a sunny, hopeful day turned into a nightmare in which he found himself on the verge of losing his moorings.

His wife was silent for a long time. He was waiting for her to say something, to absolve him, like a priest at confession. Instead, late in the afternoon, with an orange ball of sun setting over the concession stand at the far end of the beach, she grabbed a handful of sand and threw it in his face. Now standing, swimming cap in one hand and towel in the other, she walked down the beach, out of sight, out of mind.

Years

Every three years there would be an opening. Spector and his wife would go, exchange a few polite remarks with the increasingly successful painter—an old grad school buddy of Spector's—and leave. They came with their infant the first time and also when the child was three and then six. The painter and his wife, a beautiful woman with a slight limp, had wanted to have children. But they had been as unsuccessful with that as Spector had been in his career.

To Spector, each opening exemplified what he did and didn't have. The one thing that did change was the degree of importance Spector accorded the shows—as a barometer of his condition. The year his son was nine and his friend sold his first painting to an important collector, Spector had refused to attend "another boring opening." Three years later, when his son was thriving academically, Spector noticed the crowd at the gallery was sparse. Three years after that, his friend had become an art world celebrity, while he was the father of a troubled teenager who had begun to take drugs. The year Spector's son left for college, his friend was diagnosed with colon cancer and the opening had to be canceled. It wasn't until his son was almost finished with college that he saw his old friend again. He was a graying, respected, if only slightly-known artist. This was the year Spector turned sixty, the year he realized his working life was over, his dreams a thing of the past.

Usually Spector left saying, "Thanks for inviting us." To which his friend would respond with the pro forma, "You look great." But this time his friend asked, "What's it like to have a kid? I've always wanted to know."

"What's it like to be successful?" Spector countered.

Spector surprised himself with the crudeness of the response. His friend's comment had been so honest it caught him off guard, allowing the envy he had previously concealed to escape. Despite his success, his friend was far less competitive. It had never occurred to him to compare what each did or didn't have. He didn't see life as the duel Spector did. All at once Spector emerged from the obscurity of the crowd of admirers, his motives revealed. His relation to the artist was clear. Spector's friend was whisked off by his dealer to meet a wealthy collector before there was time to say anything else. Three more years passed.

The openings had become an important part of Spector's unconscious time clock. When he failed to receive an invitation to the next one, he noted it with surprise. Figuring the card had gotten lost in the mails, he looked the opening up in the paper and went.

It was a retrospective. Seeing his friend's work and the crowds it now attracted, Spector realized his rival had achieved everything anyone could want. He was being lionized. The pain would not have been so acute if his friend hadn't acted so coolly.

Spector's wife, who had a habit of explaining things away,

said, "He's just so busy, he doesn't realize what he's doing. He doesn't even know we're here." But Spector knew something had changed. And he was right. It took three more years to prove his point, and as strange as it might seem, there were few moments in the three years when Spector wasn't thinking about whether he would receive a notice for the next show. Spector was now an old man. This time when an invitation didn't arrive, he couldn't blame the mails.

Thrilled
to Death

Following the divorce, Spector sat in his living room slumped in the armchair, with its worn olive fabric, he had bought at a thrift shop. (His wife had taken all the other furniture, which was in better condition.) He felt alone and worthless—his bridges all burned behind him. Over the years, he had lost all his friends. She had been his last link to life. The unutterable loneliness of his predicament would be followed by a thrill, thoughts of the pleasures of the evening that awaited him: exotic dancers on the stage of a Chinatown strip club, lonely women languorously walking home from work on the forlorn and deserted side streets, where anything was possible. Though life was mysterious and impenetrable, a quick hookup was no further away than the time it took to pluck bills from his wallet. It was odd how these pleasurable thoughts came at moments of worthlessness and even more odd that the sensuality was so tied to a longing for oblivion. What other word was there for the seedy hotels whose flashing neon signs hung right outside the windows. Prostitutes undressing before him in shadows. He was not only escaping from his self, he was eradicating it. Drowning in stimulation, he extinguished the personality that so tormented him. Sometimes he came home hurt, beaten around the arms and legs. One morning he woke up unable to remember how he got home. Once he even found bruises, and blood on his penis.

In his more idealistic days, Spector looked at sex as the consummation of love between two people. He was loved; he loved another. He had intermittent affairs predicated on erotic desire: the attraction to a face, to lips, to breasts. But it was only at the end of the marriage when he could no longer look at himself in the mirror that sensuality and love became separated. He was unable to live with anyone; he was unable to live with himself. Love had vanished from his life, yet the erotic didn't leave him. It floated hazily over his existence—a force composed of the memories of all the sexual experiences he'd ever had, growing, compounding each minute, like interest in the bank. Disembodied torsos, genitals, groans turned his consciousness into a fragmented cubist landscape.

Lately he'd become scared. He said to himself, "Death will put an end to this pain. What am I afraid of?" But he had an animal desire to live that he couldn't account for. "If I'm going to die, I might as well have a good time" was counterbalanced by "I can't believe what I just did to myself." He would walk for hours through districts of abandoned buildings where unimaginably beautiful transvestite prostitutes, with equally unimaginable diseases, lurked. The right one, the most beautiful of the lot, the one he could not resist would be his executioner. It would start to rain. He would go home. The water would soak through the soles of his shoes.

"Thrilled to death."

That was the expression for it. He was thrilled to death.

Winter
Light

Every day Spector lingered just a little longer in his office, waiting for the excited voice of his wife, calling to tell him the letter he'd been waiting for had arrived—the letter that would change everything for him, for them. Walking home along the park, as the last leaves of autumn were blown from the trees, he superstitiously negotiated himself over every line and crack, staring at the reflection of the street lamps in the puddles that had accumulated in the crannies and potholes.

He knew if he hadn't heard from her by late afternoon, it was unlikely there would be any further messages between the time he got on the downtown local at 6:00 and arrived home at 6:30. Still he hoped, beyond hope.

He saw her coming to answer the front door in a flowery summer cocktail dress, even though it was November.

"It's come, my darling," she would say, throwing her arms around his neck, gazing up at him adoringly. "Let's celebrate."

As he opened the front door—the apartment's silence and darkness only mitigated by a shaft of light emanating from the bedroom—he would have one final spurt of hope. In this confabulation, it was a surprise party. There would be a groaning board with roast beef and turkey, chefs in high white hats, and a host of old friends crowding around him, straining to pat him on the back. Instead, he would find the bleak reality of his wife, lying curled up in a fetal position on the bed, the three-way light bulb turned to its dimmest 25-watt position, the lavish buffet of his imagination belied by the naked stove-top—an empty appliance that was at the same time sparkling clean. Yes, the worse things got, the more fastidious his wife became. Not a spot of dust, not a crumb to be found. She was a furtive person; dirt was something she spent her life trying to avoid.

As the autumn of the tenth year of their marriage passed into winter, Spector's hopes blossomed in the face of a situation which was rapidly deteriorating. The telephone calls he imagined receiving, as he sat paralyzed in his office, darkness coming earlier each day, conveyed increasingly better news. It was never a specific piece of news. For even at age forty-one, Spector wasn't sure what he wanted out of life. Money? Fame? Admiration? Respect?

The fantasies were all conveyed by way of the effect he imagined his success having on his wife. An uncharacteristic breathlessness and excitement overtook her normally controlled, sedate, cynical personality. All of a sudden this scornful presence became animated. He saw his good fortune transforming her. Daydreaming, his wife came back to him the way she was that first time he spotted her across the room at a New Year's Day party—a fresh cheery creature, just coming into her own. A breath of fresh air, he had called her. She had made him feel clean and pure after years spent cruising bars for tawdry one night stands.

Then one day in the middle of December, when the fantasied reception took the form of waiters dressed in Santa Claus costumes, he arrived to find the house in total darkness. When he turned on the lights, he saw all the furniture in the kitchen and living room was gone. Frantic, he ran to their bedroom. The mattress was still there but the Victorian bedframe was not, nor were the clothes in her closet, the expensive Ralph Lauren sheets and quilts, the antique standing lamps. He ran to the guest room, which was also emptied. With the exception of the mattress, the apartment was swept so bare it looked like it had never been lived in. He marveled at the great job she had done, before breaking down in tears.

Good
Times

Spector lived for the day he would prove himself to all the people who had ever disdained him. But when the day finally came—midway in the journey of life—they were all either dead or so destroyed that there was hardly anyone left to impress. What was it all for? The acclaim he was receiving was nothing but a ruse, a come-on. Though his name was mentioned in all the society columns and his bank account was larger by several zeros, he found things hadn't changed a bit. Fame was the invention of publicists for the benefit of all those who ever dreamt of a magical kingdom. After Spector had arrived, celebrating his induction into the inner sanctum of one of America's most exclusive clubs at the top of a skyscraper overlooking Central Park, he had left feeling as alone as he ever had before. Descending the elevator to street level, it was as if the bubble momentarily insulating him from the vicissitudes of fate—as glasses of champagne had been raised—had burst.

The way he had envisioned it was explosive. He would

reveal his good fortune to all the people who had ever spoken disparagingly of him. They would cringe. He would watch them alternately gasping for air and begging forgiveness. *How could we have so underestimated you?* But now those whose approval he always craved (a long list that stretched from early childhood on through his failed marriage) seemed pathetic, aging flesh, barely hiding the death mask's importunate eyes.

In one case, a beloved college professor—a man who always favored Spector's arch-rival—had lost his mind. When Spector called, the professor's wife was delighted, claiming how happy her husband would be to see him. But it was simply an act of desperation. The professor showed no recognition of his former student when Spector visited.

The outside world was scarcely impressed with Spector's success, but why should it be? His peers were all just like him—men reaping the fruits of many years of compulsive effort. There was no escaping. He couldn't run back to his old life. It no longer existed. Yet the present offered none of the vindication he had wished for in all the years of striving.

Besides money, attendance at charity functions seemed to be the most glaring change in Spector's existence. One evening, he bolted out of The Plaza during a particularly monotonous affair. It was nine o'clock on a Monday in early December. The first Christmas trees were just beginning to go up along Park Avenue. Slogging through the isolated years of an unhappy first marriage, Spector had always anticipated the day when the holiday season would bring invitations to elegant festivities. Now there wasn't enough time to attend all the parties he had to appear at, each more insipid than the other, with the same celebrities, celebrity caterers, and foods. He had been to the Chinese buffet with the Peking duck, the Indian dinner with the samosas, and the Japanese banquet with its opulent carousel of sushi.

...descending the Great White Way,
in search of the good times!

As he passed the corner of 59th Street and Seventh Avenue, a voice from a doorway whispered, "Going out, mister?" He turned to find a blonde in a miniskirt, shivering in a doorway. She was thin and pale, her cheeks and forehead covered with a light acne. The tight-fitting skirt only accentuated her skeletal form. In the old days Spector got drunk at the few parties he was invited to and often ended up spending his last few dollars on street prostitutes. It was ironic. Now that he could afford it, even the girls seemed worse. With nothing out of his grasp, everything had lost its allure.

He stared down Seventh Avenue at the neon signs of Times Square. Feeling a nostalgia for the old longing, he began descending the Great White Way, in search of the good times.

The
Pill

Nothing ever happened. There were lots of insights, but nothing amazing occurred. At best life was boring, at worst disappointing and downright depressing. Spector wanted something dramatic that would make him feel differently about himself. He was tired of the slow process of life. He needed an antidote to his existence, an elixir that would take effect fast.

He stared at the pill in the palm of his hand before enclosing it in his fist. The friend who had given the pill to him smiled "you'll see," when Spector expressed his chronic cynicism about anything making a difference.

Something did happen in the eight hours that followed. Indeed it was dramatic, since Spector couldn't remember any of it. Amnesia was the stuff of Hollywood movies. Like some character in a thriller, he wandered the streets not knowing who he was or recollecting afterward where he had been. If only there were some way to enjoy it. The experience was everything he wanted: powerful, out of the ordinary, spectacular enough to take him out of himself. Despite the drawback of not being able to remember it, he had accomplished his goal—a source of satisfaction in itself.

The only problem was that once it was over, it was back to business as usual: work, exercise, visits to his therapist. Something dramatic had occurred in taking a pill that made him forget his life, but nothing had changed. He could take another one. However, it turned out there was even a predictability to amnesia.

"So what," Spector found himself thinking. "So what if I can't remember."

The periods of forgetfulness and disorientation were no longer so exciting. He was restless again. Though his friend mentioned another drug, he couldn't be enticed. Day by day what had seemed dramatic was losing its romance. He still couldn't recall what happened, but the coming out of it—which felt so much like a triumph at first—now seemed tawdry at best. He saw himself a sick, pathetic creature, waking up on the floor, his clothes strewn everywhere, scratches covering his arms and legs. Yes, something out of the ordinary had happened. He had taken a pill and all at once something had changed. Yet the transformation no longer seemed so great.

Hit

List

Spector had a hit list. People he hated. People he wanted dead. He killed them over and over in his head. There were three who actually died, of natural causes. But it didn't put an end to the murder; he went on killing them day after day, in his mind, like one of those serial killers who goes on stabbing at the lifeless body. There was always murder in his dreams. Waking up, with nothing changed, his victims had come back to life, taunting him with their flagrant disregard for his murderous thoughts.

One morning, still raging from a telephone conversation with his ex-wife, Spector went further. Instead of merely wishing her demise, he began to imagine what she would look like dead. He saw the face devoid of flesh: the protruding chin, the large teeth, the high forehead and cheekbones. Seeing her as a skull, he felt a sense of sorrow for the first time. The inflammatory words, the haughtiness were gone. She was reduced to pure, clean bone. The fleshless skull with its hollow eyes is the most vulnerable of objects—the moment he envisioned his wife's, he stopped wanting to kill her. In fact, he stopped hating her entirely. The skull, which had endured, was the real person. The brain with all its nastiness was ephemeral. The cloying voice he heard the night before was just an aberration, a growth, a tumor in the cranial cavity. With the death of the body, it had disintegrated into the oblivion from which it came. So much for the eternal soul!

In this way, Spector began to bury the hatchet. He went down his hit list, reducing each of those on it to a lifeless skull. Before he knew it, the resentment which preyed upon him left. He woke in the morning with no hate for his enemies, or himself. Freed from his enervating thoughts, he found himself working more efficiently. Before he was harried and rushed, now he had time on his hands. A list of projects supplanted the hit list. He felt like a lucky man. He felt like someone who had received an anonymous gift. He wanted to live.

spector had a hit list...

The
Dead

On his last night on earth, Spector's second wife had a dinner party. She had successfully invited several "name guests" who were a step above his usual humdrum crowd. In fact, none of the old standbys, who would have joked pleasantly with Spector and made his last hours on earth comfortable, were invited at all. They were an embarrassment to Spector's wife.

The most coveted of the guests was a woman named Chantal, the born out of wedlock daughter of an art critic whose reputation had been made in the Sixties. Besides her father's name, a household word to an increasingly smaller coterie, Chantal's calling cards were her illegitimacy and her English accent. It was no wonder she hated London so. There she was like everyone else (and there were lots of bastards in England too). But in New York, she was an exotic bird indeed. No one knew how she afforded her elegant designer clothes. Some said she was kept. Others speculated she was a prostitute. All the mystery only served to make her a high ticket item. She was now part of the affluent society her father, a Marxist, had despised. And she freely took advantage of the appearance of her name in gossip columns. For days Spector's wife's anxiety about her husband's declining condition had been transferred to the prospect of the party, which she saw opening new doors.

Though Spector had never met Chantal, he already hated her. All his wife spoke of was Chantal, Chantal, Chantal.

"Chantal loves anemones, Chantal has a thing for crystals, Chantal hates Japanese mushrooms."

As he lay prostrate in the same recliner he rested in every day, he dreamt only of the final act of success, which would take the limelight away from Chantal and redeem him in his wife's eyes. The heart disease from which Spector suffered had exhausted him. He spent most of his dying days dreaming. His nightmare was the realization he didn't have the strength to undertake anything. Nevertheless, he hoped, as the evening of the dinner party approached, he would be able to rally. In his last hours, Spector was just as he had always been, full of hope and waiting for the person, thing, happenstance that would change everything.

The
Afterlife

Spector's expectations were shattered from the first day of his afterlife. It was like one of those sci-fi stories about life going on in a parallel universe. Everything was the same. His best friend was still the successful manipulator, doing the terrible things everyone loved him for; the self-haters, like himself, whose angry attitudes became a self-fulfilling prophecy, were still standing like wallflowers at social gatherings; and those born with a generosity of spirit went on giving without expecting much in return. The only difference was, it all went on for eternity. As the weeks, months, years went by, everyone became more of what they had been on earth. Spector again found himself descending into an abyss of self-pity. The more he insulted the very people he wanted to gain the attention of, the more the happiness and success of his best friend grew. In the afterlife, everyone was the epitome of their earthly being. Why not? They had forever to do it in. There was no heaven, hell, or purgatory. Dante was wrong. Everyone went on quintessentializing themselves.

Heaven…hell, it was all a state of mind.

The afterlife was the greatest disappointment of Spector's life. He had frequently quelled his envy of his best friend by saying to himself, "One day we'll all be reduced to the same pile of bones. Ashes to ashes, dust to dust." But it wasn't that way. The egalitarianism he had looked forward to didn't exist. In fact, the afterlife was a lot worse. It went on forever, containing no hope of another condition into which to escape. In life, at least you had death.

It must have been two or three thousand years into his afterlife that Spector began psychoanalysis. The psychoanalysis of the dead soul is, of course, far more complex than that of the living person. There were two lives to deal with, and then there was the question of time. Analysis was always a considerable commitment, but now when they said, "Analysis takes forever," they meant it. Indeed, the typical analyst in the afterlife was a queer bird. The one Spector chose, Dr. Mann, was a grizzled creature with huge eyeballs that never seemed to be looking at anything. And books. Rather than fifty or a hundred years of analytic texts and quarterlies, you were talking about offices filled with thousands of years worth of literature. Dr. Mann's books occupied a space equivalent to the stacks of the 42nd Street Library. Yes, everything in the afterlife was bigger, grander than things on earth. It was all like a stage set. Extinction turned out to be a groundless fear. Instead of disintegration or deterioration, everything was larger than life.

The beginning of analytic work was a turning point for Spector. Just as he had all the time in the world to get worse, the possibilities for renewal seemed endless. He kept getting better and better as the centuries passed. Soon he would surpass his best friend. There was none of the "you don't have

Dr. Mann's books occupied a space equivalent to
the stacks of the Forty-Second Street Library.

a lifetime to do it in" business that so aggravated his self-destructiveness in life. With an eternity before him and little more at risk than things worsening again, self-undoing lost its allure. Sure, there was no limit to the depths you could reach, but after a thousand years people forgot, and with another century of therapy they looked at you in a completely different light. "Death is good," Spector said to himself one day after a session.

There were, of course, frustrations. While the infinitely bad could be turned into the infinitely good, certain immutable laws governed death as well as life. He would, for instance, still not be able to sleep with his mother and it was unlikely he would be invited to his analyst's house for dinner. But that itself was a recognition. After thousands of years of psychoanalysis, one of the most important signs of Spector's growth was his realization that you can't have everything.

About the Author
and Illustrator

Francis Levy is the author of the comic novels *Erotomania: A Romance* (Two Dollar Radio, 2008) and *Seven Days in Rio* (Two Dollar Radio, 2011). He is also the author of *Tombstone: Not a Western* (Black Rose, 2018). Levy's first novel, *Erotomania: A Romance*, evoked critical comparisons to the work of Charles Bukowski, Henry Miller, Mary Gaitskill and D. H. Lawrence. *The New York Times* called his second novel, *Seven Days in Rio*, "a fever dream of a novel" and *The Village Voice* wrote: "The funniest American novel since Sam Lipsyte's *The Ask*." Levy has been profiled in *The East Hampton Star*, *AIGA Voice*, *Nerve*, *Interview*, and elsewhere. Follow his blog at **screamingpope.com**.

Hallie Cohen received her M.F.A. from the Hoffberger School of Painting of the Maryland Institute College of Art, where she studied with the painter Grace Hartigan. She is Professor of Art and Director of the Hewitt Gallery at Marymount Manhattan College.

Printed in the USA
CPSIA information can be obtained
at www.ICGtesting.com
JSHW072352100823
46350JS00009B/149